LIFE IS FUN

BY NANCY CARLSON

VIKING

To Lucia,
who is a great cook
and my running, biking,
swimming buddy.

VIKING
Published by the Penguin Group
Penguin Books USA Inc., 375 Hudson Street, New York, New York 10014, U.S.A.
Penguin Books Ltd, 27 Wrights Lane, London W8 5TZ, England
Penguin Books Australia Ltd, Ringwood, Victoria, Australia
Penguin Books Canada Ltd, 10 Alcorn Avenue, Toronto, Ontario, Canada M4V 3B2
Penguin Books (N.Z.) Ltd, 182–190 Wairau Road, Auckland 10, New Zealand

Penguin Books Ltd, Registered Offices: Harmondsworth, Middlesex, England

First published in 1993 by Viking, a division of Penguin Books USA Inc.

1   3   5   7   9   10   8   6   4   2

Life can be fun . . .
(Really, it can!)

THIS IS EARTH.

You live here.

To be happy on Earth,
FOLLOW THESE
SIMPLE INSTRUCTIONS!

1. BE NICE TO OTHERS

Be nice to your little sister,

and to your pets.

Be nice to the nerdy kid next door,

and to any space creatures you may meet.

2. BE NICE TO YOURSELF

Order yourself a triple-scoop ice cream cone.

Don't worry about stuff!

Sleep late!

And if you feel like crying,

CRY!

3. BE HEALTHY

Keep fit.

Eat food that's good for you once in a while.

Remember to wash your ears.

4. STAY OUT OF TROUBLE IN SCHOOL

Study real hard.

Keep away from the tough guys.

5. STAY OUT OF TROUBLE AT HOME

Don't bring snakes inside.

Keep your room clean.

SNAIL LAKE SCHOOL, IMC
4550 Hodgson Road
St. Paul, MN 55126

6. HAVE FUN

Tell jokes.

Laugh a lot!

Fall in love.

7. DO YOUR OWN THING

Go barefoot.

Sing loud!

Dress real cool.

Relax and go fishing.

Watch clouds go by and

make big, big plans.

So while you're on Earth,
do these things and
you will be . . .

AWESOME!

SNAIL LAKE SCHOOL, IMC
4550 ~~Hodgson Road~~
St. Paul, MN 55126

Turtle Lake Elementary School
1141 Lepak Court
Shoreview, MN 55126-5698